For
Bobbi-Dazzler
xxx

The Tiny Tree © 2015 by Allan Plenderleith
For more books by Allan visit allanplenderleith.com

First published in 2015
by
Ravette Publishing Limited
PO Box 876, Horsham, West Sussex RH12 9GH

ISBN: 978-1-84161-392-5

The Tiny Tree

by Allan Plenderleith

RAVETTE PUBLISHING

Deep, deep down in the dark, dark woods
stood a tiny pine tree.

The tree was the tiniest tree in the whole forest and all she could do was look up at the other trees and dream.

She wished one day to be a
Christmas tree, dressed from tip to trunk
in the finest decorations,
surrounded by laughter and love.

But the other big trees thought she was being silly.

"Don't be daft! No one wants a tiny tree! They want a big tall tree like me!" said one of the big tall trees.

When she awoke, the tiny tree looked around.
"Phew! I'm alive!" she said relieved.
"But wait - where am I?"

Then she realised where she was -
on the back of a truck with all the other trees!
She had been chopped down by mistake!

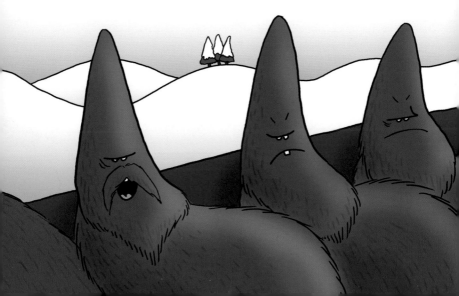

But maybe someone WOULD
pick her to be their
Christmas tree, she dreamed.
"Maybe MY Christmas
will come too!"

The truck finally arrived in the city,
which was covered in Christmas decorations.
Everything twinkled!

The truck stopped at a market stall,
and all the trees were
loaded off onto the pavement.

And he threw the tiny tree to one side.

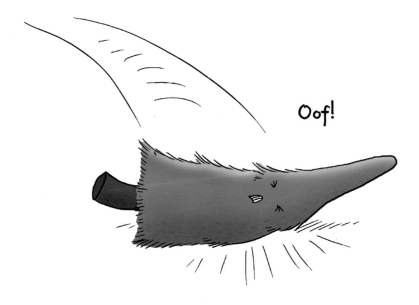

But the tiny tree thought
the tree seller was wrong.
"Maybe someone DOES want
a tree as tiny as me.
I'll show them."

So she stood next to all the other trees, standing on a bucket to get some extra height.

But everyone ignored her.
They went straight past the tiny tree
and picked a big tree to take home.
It was like she was invisible.

Soon, the tiny tree was the only tree left.

The shop keeper shut up shop and went home,
leaving the little tree all alone.

She walked along the busy streets as people
bustled and bashed with
their big bags of Christmas shopping.

Then she saw something.

A shop window with the most
beautiful Christmas tree,
filled with bright lights,
shiny baubles and twinkly tinsel.

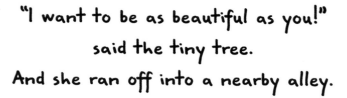

"I want to be as beautiful as you!"
said the tiny tree.
And she ran off into a nearby alley.

After a minute or two she appeared, dressed from tip to trunk in litter! It was all she could find but the tiny tree thought she looked beautiful.

"Now I'm sure someone will want me for their Christmas tree!" she said, and ran back into the street full of excitement.

The first thing people noticed
was the smell - it was not a good smell.
It was a bad smell.
Definitely not pine fresh.

"Please - can I be your Christmas tree?"
said the tiny tree.

"Aaargh! No thanks!"
screamed the shoppers, running from the stinky stench.

Soon the street was empty.

The tiny tree walked the
quiet streets all alone.

Until...

She saw the most beautiful thing she
had ever seen - a GIANT Christmas tree,
taller than a building!
And underneath, was Father Christmas!

She ran up to him
and said
"Father Christmas!
Father Christmas!
Please can I be YOUR
Christmas tree?"

Father Christmas bent down and picked up the tiny tree in his arms. He looked at her and said...

"Certainly not, you stinky stick, the only place you're good for is the bin!"

And with that, he threw her into a passing rubbish truck!

The tiny tree had a feeling that WASN'T the real Father Christmas.

The truck passed through the streets
on towards the dump.
The tiny tree shed a tiny tear.

There she was tipped out with
the rest of the rubbish.
"No one wants me
for their Christmas tree..."
she sobbed.

But then she heard some strange sounds...
A skittering, a scuttling,
a shuffling, a snuffling.
A squeak, a tweet, a chirp, a cheep!

It was a little mouse, a squirrel, and a robin.
They had followed the tiny tree
all the way from the forest!

The little mouse spoke first.
"Little tree, little tree -
can you be OUR Christmas tree?"

The tiny tree was amazed.
"You want ME to be your Christmas tree?"

Suddenly a flock of robins flew
over to the tiny tree!

The robins lifted her up as the mouse
and squirrel hopped on,
and flew her all the way back to the forest!

When they arrived she was decorated
in acorn baubles, winter flowers and holly tinsel!

They looked up at the tree
who to them was
the biggest, brightest, most beautiful
thing they had ever seen!

And the tiny tree's Christmas had
come at last, dressed from
tip to trunk in the finest decorations,
surrounded by laughter...

...and love.

The end.

More Christmas books by Allan Plenderleith:

The Christmas Carrot

Everyone wants a piece of me!

by Allan Plenderleith

The Bonkers Banana

by Allan Plenderleith

The Silly Satsuma

What can a silly satsuma do?

by Allan Plenderleith

The Smelly Sprout

Why does nobody like me?

by Allan Plenderleith

Complete your collection!

allanplenderleith.com